by J.E.
Bright

HEROES
OF THE
HIGH SEAS

illustrated by
Art Baltazar

Picture Window Books
a capstone imprint

TABLE OF CONTENTS!

ATLANTIS HIGH COMMAND
SEA COMPUTER

STORM

Ultra Smart

Mind Communication

Underwater Breathing

Aqua Belt

Horsepower

4

Super Hero Owner:
AQUAMAN

Species: Giant Seahorse

Place of Birth: Atlantis

Age: Unknown

Favorite Foods:
Shrimp and seaweed

Bio: When Aquaman needs a lift, he calls his superpowered seahorse. With the Sea King on his back, Storm can sail beneath the sea or ride atop the waves at super-speed. He's a pretty good dancer, too!

Chapter 1

WILD WHIRLPOOL!

Topo the Octopus loved playing music for his friend, Aquaman, the king of the underwater city of Atlantis.

Today, Topo entertained the royal court with a lively tune. He played the drums, the trumpet, and the banjo with his eight tentacles.

Aquaman smiled. He nodded his head to the music. Topo was glad he could make the Sea King forget his royal troubles for a while.

BARK! BARK!

Suddenly, Topo's concert was stopped. A seal named Ark rushed into the throne room.

"My king!" Ark shouted. "Red alert! The city is in terrible danger!"

"Explain," Aquaman commanded.

Ark quickly swam to the throne.

"A giant whirlpool has erupted in the Triton Trench," shouted the seal. "It's growing bigger every minute!"

Topo shivered with worry. The Triton Trench was located far below the city of Atlantis. Few had ever visited the trench's dark depths.

"I can't have my city destroyed," Aquaman said. "We must investigate!"

The Sea King focused hard. In moments, a seahorse named **Storm** burst into the throne room. He had answered Aquaman's silent command.

"Hop on, sire!" Storm trumpeted.

The seahorse was more than twice the size of Aquaman. He was one of the fastest steeds in the underwater world.

Aquaman leaped onto his back.

"Ark, Topo, follow me!" he ordered.

Ark sped after Aquaman. Topo quickly grabbed his violin and bow. The instrument could play beautiful music. It could also be used as a weapon. Then Topo followed his master toward the palace exit.

Once outside, Aquaman led his pets along the city streets. People cheered as they saw the Sea King race past. The fish and folk of the undersea city were used to seeing their king hurry away on heroic missions. Still, Topo felt thrilled by their roar of praise.

Topo couldn't swim as fast as Ark or Storm. He grabbed onto the seahorse's tail. He held tight as Storm carried Aquaman into the wild ocean outside Atlantis. **WOOOOSH!**

Right away, Topo spotted the funnel. It swirled out of the Triton Trench. The funnel grew wider as it churned toward the ocean surface. **It looked like a giant underwater tornado.**

Topo the octopus held on tightly. Storm the seahorse charged closer toward the spinning vortex.

Storm stopped at the edge of the trench. Up close, Topo saw that the whirlpool was getting larger. It was growing with bursts of power.

Topo let go of Storm and looked into the trench. He could feel the strength of the whirlpool pulling at him. He clung to rocks with his tentacles.

The vortex swirled downward. It disappeared into the depths of the trench. The dirty water hid any clue to the funnel's source.

"If the whirlpool gets much larger, it will destroy the city!" said Aquaman.

"Sire, look!" Ark called. He pointed a flipper toward the surface. A giant creature was struggling against the powerful funnel.

A female blue whale had been caught in the swirling water. She was trying with all her might not to be sucked down into the trench.

"Gasp!" The octopus saw that the blue whale wasn't alone. She was swimming against the vortex, trying to keep her young calf safe.

MOOANNNN!

The blue whale let out a sad cry.

She and her calf began to slip deeper into the vortex. They were losing their battle against the whirlpool.

Aquaman leaped off Storm. He swam toward the whale and her baby.

"I'll help them," the Sea King called to his Super-Pets. "You three go down the trench. **Find out what's causing the vortex, and stop it!"**

Chapter 2

INTO THE DEEP

The Super-Pets dived into the deep, dark trench. Topo rode atop Storm. Ark swam alongside. They all kept close to the rock wall so the vortex didn't suck them in.

As they went deeper into the trench, the vortex got bigger and bigger.

Topo worried they wouldn't reach the bottom before the funnel filled the trench. It would rip apart the cliff that held Atlantis.

"Faster!" Topo told Storm.

"Hold your seahorses! I'm swimming as fast as I can," Storm replied. The seahorse kicked his tail hard. He quickly reached full speed.

The bottom of the trench was still far away. The funnel disappeared into the muddy water below.

A glowing jellyfish swirled past inside the vortex. It spiraled down the funnel faster than Storm was swimming. The jellyfish wriggled in fear. **SHHIVVERR!**

"Maybe we should ride the vortex," Topo suggested. **"We have to get down there now!"**

Ark the seal smacked his flippers together. **"Let's do it!"** he barked.

"Giddy-up!" Storm shouted. He darted toward the bubbling funnel.

Topo clung to the seahorse as the vortex snatched them into its wild swirl. Storm spiraled out of control. He turned upside down, backward, flipping over again.

The vortex tumbled the Super-Pets along its spinning chute. Ark suddenly shot past the seahorse. He was pulled down the watery tornado.

Topo reached out a tentacle. He wrapped it around Ark's tail. **They needed to stick together.**

"**Keep swimming!**" Topo yelled at Storm. "We won't be tossed around so much if you swim along the swirl!"

The seahorse gave his tail a quick thrust. **THWAP!** With Storm wriggling his powerful body, the pets rode the whipping water downward.

Topo peered out at the sides of the trench swirling past. Up ahead, near the sandy bottom, the vortex suddenly arched sideways. "Push out!" Topo screamed. "Don't follow the funnel! **Dive to the sand!**"

Storm pushed through the funnel's wall. At the curve where the vortex turned, the pets jumped free.

They smacked down on the ocean floor. **THUD!** Topo's head was spinning. He had managed to hold onto Ark's tail during the ride.

"Talk about sea sickness!" Topo said with a laugh. **"My head is swimming."**

Through his dizziness, Topo saw that the vortex was coming out of a lava tunnel. The tunnel was located in the side of the trench. The volcano that had created the mountain under Atlantis was long extinct. Still, the rock was dotted with old lava tunnels.

Something inside the tunnels was causing the vortex. Topo led Storm and Ark toward it to take a closer look.

The Super-Pets followed the tunnel until they reached a cave. Topo spotted a light glowing ahead. Then he heard a strange grinding sound.

"What is that?!" the octopus said. He swam closer to the light.

The light was coming from a strange sea creature. The animal looked like a hugely fat grub. It had a glowing spot on its forehead.

"It's a diggler!" Topo shouted.

Topo had never seen a diggler up close. They were very rare. The animal usually spent its life tunneling through the ocean bed, looking for food. They were known to be gentle and harmless. But this one seemed ready to attack.

"Why is it tunneling into the mountain?" Ark asked. "Is it lost?"

"I don't know," Topo replied. **But then he saw why the diggler was acting so strangely.**

By the light of the diggler's glowing spot, Topo could see **two large manta rays** poking the poor creature. They dived down at it, snapping their tails. The diggler let out a squeal.

"I know those mantas," Topo said.

"Me too," Ark whispered. **"Misty and Sneezers!"**

"Black Manta's pets," Topo added quietly. "Up to no good."

Black Manta was Aquaman's worst enemy. He always tried to steal the ocean's treasures or destroy Atlantis.

Topo sneaked closer to watch Misty and Sneezers bother the diggler. They made the creature dig more. When the diggler broke through the rock, water rushed into the empty lava tubes.

As water flowed into these tubes, it began to swirl like a flushing toilet. That was causing the vortex!

"Just a few more tubes," Misty growled. "Then the vortex will cause the whole cliff to crumble, taking Atlantis with it!" She laughed nastily.

"Uh . . . Yeah!" Sneezers agreed.

"No," Topo said firmly. **"That's not going to happen."**

Chapter 3

SOUNDS OF VICTORY

Misty and Sneezers whirled around.

Their eyes widened when they saw the

Super-Pets standing in front of them.

"If it isn't Aquaman's little pets,"

Misty sneered.

"Yeah," Sneezers added.

"We're bigger than you!" Ark said.

"The only size that matters," Misty replied, "is the size of the vortex!"

She spanked the diggler on the rump. The tunneling creature sped toward the next tunnel in the rock. "This last tunnel will make the vortex big enough to destroy Atlantis!"

"Stop the mantas!" Topo told his friends. **"I'll stop the diggler!"**

Ark and Storm rushed at the evil manta rays. Ark spun around and whapped Sneezers with his tail.

Storm did the same to Misty and sent her spiraling away. The mantas soared back, trying to bite again.

While his friends were busy with the battle, Topo tried to figure out how to stop the diggler.

Usually digglers were peaceful. The mantas had made this one angry and out of control. If only Topo could calm the diggler's anger.

"Music soothes the savage beast," Topo whispered. The octopus whipped out his violin and started to play.

Topo kept the music slow and tried to relax the diggler. At first, it didn't seem to be working. But as Ark and Storm forced Misty and Sneezers farther away from the diggler, the music began to have a soothing effect.

The diggler slowed his tunneling. His body relaxed. He turned to look with tiny eyes at Topo.

The diggler still had his teeth showing. They were sharp enough to bite through solid rock. **The octopus played a long note on the violin.**

Finally the diggler's mouth closed. With no new tunnels opening up, the vortex's churning slowed.

"Good boy," Topo whispered. "Nobody will hurt you anymore."

Seeing what Topo had done, Misty and Sneezers tried to push past Storm and Ark to reach the diggler.

"I wouldn't," Topo said softly. **"I know polka music as well."**

"Yikes! Let's get out of here!" Misty yelped.

"**Yeah!**" Sneezer added. He and Misty slipped away down the tunnel.

"**Follow them,**" Topo said. "They're probably heading toward wherever Black Manta is hiding!"

The octopus leaped onto Storm's back. They zoomed after the escaping manta rays. Topo noticed that the diggler was following, too.

Misty and Sneezer rushed along the bottom of the trench. Topo, Storm, and Ark followed closely behind.

Then suddenly the mantas ducked behind a large, oval rock.

"We've got them cornered!" Ark cheered.

"Wait!" Topo said. **"I don't think that's a rock."**

A row of lights along the oval object flashed on, momentarily blinding everyone. **It was Black Manta's submarine!** On top of the submarine, a hatch slid open, and Black Manta's helmeted head rose out of the opening.

"Look what we have here," the villain said in his deep voice. "So you had my pets on the run, did you? **Let's see if you can handle *me*!**"

Sneezers peeked out over the top of the submarine. **"Yeah!"** he added.

Topo clung to Storm's back. He didn't doubt his friends' strength, but he knew just how dangerous Black Manta could be. Even Aquaman had struggled to defeat the villain in the past. Topo wasn't sure if they could win a battle with Black Manta.

Topo was determined to do his best to stop the villain from escaping.

Then an incredibly loud, high-pitched whine filled the trench from behind Black Manta.

Black Manta whirled around.

The fiend came face-to-face with one angry female blue whale. The whale completely dwarfed the villain.

Aquaman swam beside the blue whale. "Your vortex made this mother whale quite unhappy," Aquaman called to Black Manta. **"Maybe you should have thought twice before endangering her child."**

"Eep!" Black Manta squealed. He ducked back into his submarine. His mantas followed. The submarine took off, zooming upward.

"Go ahead," Aquaman told the blue whale. **"I'll keep an eye on your young one."**

The blue whale grinned and then shot upward. She chased the submarine out of sight. Topo had no doubt that the blue whale would scare Black Manta across the entire ocean.

"Congrats on stopping Black Manta!" Aquaman told his friends. "What was causing the vortex?"

Topo pointed a tentacle toward the diggler. **"The mantas angered this tunneler,"** the octopus said. "He didn't mean to cause so much trouble. Misty and Sneezers were driving him crazy."

"A diggler!" Aquaman said delightedly, swimming over to the grub-like creature. "I haven't seen one of those in years." He patted the diggler on the back. **"How did you calm him down?"**

Topo pulled out his drums. **"Like this,"** he said, and the octopus began to play a bouncy tune that echoed along the walls of the Triton Trench.

The baby blue whale sang along. It swam circles in the water and danced. His mother returned and joined in.

Aquaman, Storm, and Ark all joined the calf's dance as well. After a moment, the diggler wriggled in a happy jig, too.

Topo smiled. Thanks to his friends, both old and new, Atlantis was safe once again.

KNOW YOUR

 Krypto

Streaky

 Beppo

 Comet

 Ace

 Jumpa

 Whatzit

 B'dg

 Storm

 Topo

 Ark

 Hoppy

 Paw Pooch

 Bull Dog

 Chameleon Collie

 Hot Dog

Aw yeah, **HERO** PETS!

 Tail Terrier

 Tusky Husky

SUPER-PETS!

Ignatius

Chauncey

Crackers

Giggles

Artie Puffin

Griff

Waddles

Rozz

Dex-Starr

Glomulus

Misty

Sneezers

Whoosh

Pronto

Snorrt

Rolf

Squealer

Kajunn

Aw yeah, **VILLAIN PETS!**

AW YEAH, JOKES!

What do you call an outlaw octopus?

What?

Billy the squid!

What kind of horse swims under water?

Beats me.

A seahorse, of course!

What happens when you throw a blue rock into the Red Sea?

I dunno.

It sinks, silly!

WORD POWER!

extinct (ek-STINGKT)—no longer erupting

polka (POLE-kuh)—a fast dance in which couples
swirl around the floor in a circle pattern

tentacles (TEN-tuh-kuhlz)—long, flexible limbs
used by an octopus for moving, feeling, and grabbing

throne (THROHN)—a large chair for a king or queen

trench (TRENCH)—a long, narrow ditch

vortex (VOHR-teks)—a swirling body of water that
looks like an underwater tornado

MEET THE AUTHOR!

J. E. Bright

J. E. Bright has had more than 50 novels, novelizations, and non-fiction books published for children and young adults. He is a full-time freelance writer, living in a tiny apartment in the SoHo neighborhood of Manhattan with his good, fat cat, Gladys, and his evil cat, Mabel, who is getting fatter.

MEET THE ILLUSTRATOR!

Eisner Award-winner Art Baltazar

Art Baltazar is a cartoonist machine from the heart of Chicago! He defines cartoons and comics not only as an art style, but as a way of life. Currently, Art is the creative force behind *The New York Times* best-selling, Eisner Award-winning, DC Comics series Tiny Titans and the co-writer for *Billy Batson and the Magic of SHAZAM!* Art is living the dream! He draws comics and never has to leave the house. He lives with his lovely wife, Rose, big boy Sonny, little boy Gordon, and little girl Audrey. Right on!

READ THEM ALL!

DC SUPER-PETS!

THE FUN DOESN'T STOP HERE!

Discover more:

- Videos & Contests!
- Games & Puzzles!
- Heroes & Villains!
- Authors & Illustrators!

@ www.capstonekids.com

Find cool websites and more books like this one at www.facthound.com Just type in Book I.D. 9781404862630 and you're ready to go!

Picture Window Books™

Published in 2011
A Capstone Imprint
1710 Roe Crest Drive
North Mankato, Minnesota 56003
www.capstonepub.com

Cataloging-in-Publication Data is available at the Library of Congress website.
ISBN: 978-1-4048-6263-0 (library binding)
ISBN: 978-1-4048-6621-8 (paperback)

Summary: A huge whirlpool threatens the city of Atlantis and Topo the Octopus must come to the rescue.

Art Director & Designer: Bob Lentz
Editor: Donald Lemke
Creative Director: Heather Kindseth
Editorial Director: Michael Dahl

Printed in the United States of America in North Mankato, Minnesota.
032014   008121R